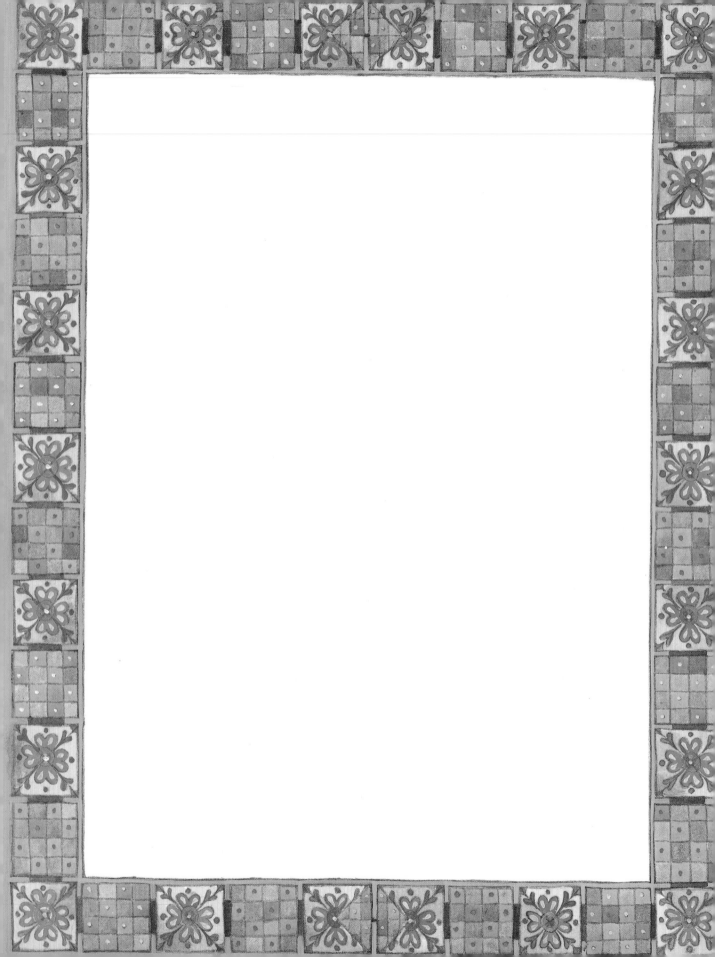

BEARSKIN

BEARSKIN

by *Howard Pyle*
illustrated by *Trina Schart Hyman*

Afterword by
Peter Glassman

BOOKS OF WONDER
MORROW JUNIOR BOOKS • NEW YORK

For everybody at Open Fields School
——T.S.H.

India ink and acrylic paints were used for the full-color illustrations.
The text type is 15/19-point Berkeley Old Style.
Illustrations copyright © 1997 by Trina Schart Hyman
Afterword copyright © 1997 by Peter Glassman
Printed in Hong Kong by South China Printing Company (1988) Ltd.
1 2 3 4 5 6 7 8 9 10

Library of Congress Cataloging-in-Publication Data
Pyle, Howard, 1853–1911.
Bearskin/by Howard Pyle; illustrated by Trina Schart Hyman.
p. cm.—(Books of Wonder)
Summary: A brave young man who has been raised by a bear with unusual powers rescues a princess from a
menacing dragon and fulfills a long-ago prophecy that he would marry the king's daughter.
ISBN 0-688-09837-1 (trade)—ISBN 0-688-09838-X (library)
[1. Fairy tales. 2. Kings, queens, rulers, etc.—Fiction.] I. Hyman, Trina Schart, ill. II. Title. III. Series.
PZ8.P991Be 1997 [Fic]—dc20 96-32451 CIP AC

*T*here was a king traveling through the country, and he and those with him were so far away from home that darkness caught them by the heels, and they had to stop at a stone mill for the night, because there was no other place handy.

While they sat at supper they heard a sound in the next room, and it was a baby crying.

The miller stood in the corner, in back of the stove, with his hat in his hand. "What is that noise?" said the king to him.

"Oh! It is nothing but another baby that the good storks have brought into the house today," said the miller.

Now, there was a wise man traveling along with the king who could read the stars and everything that they told as easily as one can read one's ABC's in a book after one knows them, and the king, for a bit of a jest, would have him find out what the stars had to foretell of the miller's baby. So the wise man went out and took a peep up in the sky, and by and by he came in again.

"Well," said the king, "and what did the stars tell you?"

"The stars tell me," said the wise man, "that you shall have a daughter, and that the miller's baby, in the room yonder, shall marry her when they are old enough to think of such things."

"What!" said the king. "And is a miller's baby to marry the princess that is to come! We will see about that." So the next day he took the miller aside and talked and bargained, and bargained and talked, until the upshot of the matter was that the miller was paid two hundred dollars and the king rode off with the baby.

As soon as he came home to the castle he called his chief forester to him. "Here," says he, "take this baby and do thus and so with it, and when you have killed it bring its heart to me, that I may know that you have really done as you have been told."

So off marched the forester with the baby; but on his way he stopped at home, and there was his good wife, working about the house.

"Well, Henry," said she, "what are you doing with the baby?"

"Oh!" said he. "I am just taking it off to the forest to do thus and so with it."

"Come," said she, "it would be a pity to harm the little innocent and to have its blood on your hands. Yonder hangs the rabbit that you shot this morning, and its heart will please the king just as well as the other."

Thus the wife talked, and the end of the business was that she and the man smeared a basket all over with pitch and set the baby adrift in it on the river, and the king was just as well satisfied with the rabbit's heart as he would have been with the baby's.

But the basket with the baby in it drifted on and on down the river, until it lodged at last among the high reeds that stood along the bank. By and by there came a great she-bear to the water to drink, and there she found it.

Now, the huntsmen in the forest had robbed the she-bear of her cubs, so that her heart yearned over the little baby, and she carried it home with her to fill the place of her own young ones. There the baby throve until he grew to a great strong lad, and as he had fed upon nothing but bear's milk for all that time, he was ten times stronger than the strongest man in the land.

One day, as he was walking through the forest, he came across a woodman chopping the trees into billets of wood, and that was the first time he had ever seen a body like himself. Back he went to the bear as fast as he could travel and told her what he had seen. "That," said the bear, "is the most wicked and most cruel of all the beasts."

"Yes," says the lad, "that may be so. All the same I love beasts like that as I love the food I eat, and I long for nothing so much as to go out into the wide world, where I may find others of the same kind."

At this the bear saw very well how the geese flew, and that the lad would soon be flitting.

"See," said she, "if you must go out into the wide world, you must. But you will be wanting help before long; for the ways of the world are not peaceful and simple as they are here in the woods, and before you have lived there long you will have more needs than there are flies in summer. See, here is a little crooked horn, and when your wants grow many, just come to the forest and blow a blast on it, and I will not be too far away to help you."

So off went the lad away from the forest, and all the coat he had upon his back was the skin of a bear dressed with the hair on it, and that was why folk called him "Bearskin."

He trudged along the high road until he came to the king's castle, and it was the same king who thought he had put Bearskin safe out of the way years and years ago.

Now, the king's swineherd was in want of a lad, and as there was nothing better to do in that town, Bearskin took the place and went every morning to help drive the pigs into the forest, where they might eat the acorns and grow fat.

One day there was a mighty stir throughout the town: folk crying and making a great hubbub. "What is it all about?" says Bearskin to the swineherd.

What! And did he not know what the trouble was? Where had he been for all of his life that he had heard nothing of what was going on in the world? Had he never heard of the great fiery dragon with three heads that had threatened to lay waste all of that land unless the pretty princess were given up to him? This was the very day that the dragon was to come for her, and she was to be sent up on the hill in back of the town; that was why all the folk were crying and making such a stir.

"So!" says Bearskin. "And is there never a lad in the whole country that is man enough to face the beast? Then I will go myself if nobody better is to be found." And off he went, though the swineherd laughed and laughed and thought it all a bit of a jest. By and by Bearskin came to the forest, and there he blew a blast upon the little crooked horn that the bear had given him.

Presently came the bear through the bushes, so fast that the little twigs flew behind her. "And what is it that you want?" said she.

"I should like," said Bearskin, "to have a horse, a suit of gold and silver armor that nothing can pierce, and a sword that shall cut through iron and steel; for I would like to go up on the hill to fight the dragon and free the pretty princess at the king's town over yonder."

"Very well," said the bear. "Look in back of the tree yonder, and you will find just what you want."

Yes, sure enough, there they were in back of the tree: a grand white horse that champed his bit and pawed the ground till the gravel flew, and a suit of gold and silver armor such as a king might wear. Bearskin put on the armor and mounted the horse, and off he rode to the high hill in back of the town.

By and by came the princess and the steward of the castle,
for it was he who was to bring her to the dragon. But the steward stayed at the bottom of the hill, for he was afraid, and the
princess had to climb it alone, though she could hardly see
the road before her for the tears that fell from her eyes. But
when she reached the top of the hill, she found instead of the
dragon a fine tall fellow dressed all in gold and silver armor.
And it did not take Bearskin long to comfort the princess, I
can tell you. "Come, come," says he, "dry your eyes and cry
no more; all the cakes in the oven are not burned yet. Just go
in back of the bushes yonder, and leave it with me to talk the
matter over with Master Dragon."

The princess was glad enough to do that. In back of the bushes she went, and Bearskin waited for the dragon to come. He had not long to wait either, for presently it came flying through the air, so that the wind rattled under his wings.

Dear, dear! If one could but have been there to see that fight between Bearskin and the dragon, for it was well worth the seeing, and that you may believe. The dragon spit out flames and smoke like a house afire. But he could do no hurt to Bearskin, for the gold and silver armor sheltered him so well that not so much as one single hair of his head was singed. So Bearskin just rattled away the blows at the dragon—slish, slash, snip, clip—until all three heads were off, and there was an end to it.

After that he cut out the tongues from the three heads of
the dragon and tied them up in his pocket-handkerchief.

Then the princess came out from behind the bushes
where she had lain hidden and begged Bearskin to go back
with her to the king's castle, for the king had said that if any-
one killed the dragon he should have her for his wife. But no,
Bearskin would not go to the castle just now, for the time was
not yet ripe; but, if the princess would give them to him, he
would like to have the ring from her finger, the kerchief from
her bosom, and the necklace of golden beads from her neck.

The princess gave him what he asked for, and a sweet kiss into the bargain, and then Bearskin mounted upon his grand white horse and rode away to the forest. "Here are your horse and armor," said he to the bear, "and they have done good service today, I can tell you." Then he tramped back again to the king's castle with the old bear's skin over his shoulders.

"Well," says the swineherd, "and did you kill the dragon?"

"Oh, yes," says Bearskin, "I did that, but it was no such great thing to do after all."

At that the swineherd laughed and laughed, for he did not believe a word of it.

And now listen to what happened to the princess after
Bearskin had left her. The steward came sneaking up to see
how matters had turned out, and there he found her safe and
sound, and the dragon dead. "Whoever did this left his luck
behind him," said he, and he drew his sword and told the
princess that he would kill her if she did not swear to say
nothing of what had happened. Then he gathered up the
dragon's three heads, and he and the princess went back to
the castle again.

"There!" said he when they had come before the king, and he flung down the three heads upon the floor. "I have killed the dragon and I have brought back the princess, and now if anything is to be had for the labor I would like to have it." As for the princess, she wept and wept, but she could say nothing, and so it was fixed that she was to marry the steward, for that was what the king had promised.

At last came the wedding day, and the smoke went up from the chimneys in clouds, for there was to be a grand wedding feast, and there was no end of good things cooking for those who were to come.

"See now," says Bearskin to the swineherd where they were feeding their pigs together, out in the woods, "as I killed the dragon over yonder, I ought at least to have some of the good things from the king's kitchen; you shall go and ask for some of the fine white bread and meat, such as the king and princess are to eat today."

Dear, dear, but you should have seen how the swineherd stared at this and how he laughed, for he thought the other must have gone out of his wits; but as for going to the castle—no, he would not go a step, and that was the long and the short of it.

"So! Well, we will see about that," says Bearskin, and he stepped to a thicket and cut a good stout stick, and without another word caught the swineherd by the collar and began dusting his jacket for him until it smoked.

"Stop, stop!" bawled the swineherd.

"Very well," says Bearskin. "And now will you go over to the castle for me and ask for some of the same bread and meat that the king and princess are to have for their dinner?"

Yes, yes, the swineherd would do anything that Bearskin wanted him to.

"So! Good," says Bearskin. "Then just take this ring and see that the princess gets it; and say that the lad who sent it would like to have some of the bread and meat that she is to have for her dinner."

So the swineherd took the ring, and off he started to do as he had been told. Rap! Tap! Tap! He knocked at the door. Well, and what did he want?

Oh! There was a lad over in the woods yonder who had sent him to ask for some of the same bread and meat that the king and princess were to have for their dinner, and he had brought this ring to the princess as a token.

But how the princess opened her eyes when she saw the ring that she had given to Bearskin up on the hill! For she saw, as plain as the nose on her face, that he who had saved her from the dragon was not so far away as she had thought. Down she went into the kitchen herself to see that the very best bread and meat were sent, and the swineherd marched off with a great basketful.

"Yes," says Bearskin, "that is very well so far, but I am for having some of the red and white wine that they are to drink. Just take this kerchief over to the castle yonder, and let the princess know that the lad to whom she gave it upon the hill in back of the town would like to have a taste of the wine that she and the king are to have at the feast today."

Well, the swineherd was for saying no to this as he had to the other, but Bearskin just reached his hand over toward the stout stick that he had used before, and the other started off as though the ground was hot under his feet. And what was the swineherd wanting this time? That was what they said over at the castle.

"The lad with the pigs in the woods yonder," says the swineherd, "must have gone crazy, for he has sent this kerchief to the princess and says that he should like to have a bottle or two of the wine that she and the king are to drink today."

When the princess saw her kerchief again her heart leaped for joy. She made no two words about the wine but went down into the cellar and brought it up with her own hands, and the swineherd marched off with it tucked under his coat.

"Yes, that was all very well," said Bearskin. "I am satisfied so far as the wine is concerned, but now I would like to have some of the sweetmeats that they are to eat at the castle today. See, here is a necklace of golden beads; just take it to the princess and ask for some of those sweetmeats, for I will have them." And this time he had only to look toward the stick, and the other started off as fast as he could travel.

The swineherd had no more trouble with this asking than with the others, for the princess went downstairs and brought the sweetmeats from the pantry with her own hands, and the swineherd carried them to Bearskin where he sat out in the woods with the pigs.

Then Bearskin spread out the good things, and he and the swineherd sat down to the feast together, and a fine one it was, I can tell you.

"And now," says Bearskin when they had eaten all that they could, "it is time for me to leave you, for I must go and marry the princess." So off he started, and the swineherd did nothing but stand and gape after him with his mouth open, as though he were set to catch flies. But Bearskin went straight to the woods, and there he blew upon his horn, and the bear was with him as quickly this time as the last.

"Well, what do you want now?" said she.

"This time," said Bearskin, "I want a fine suit of clothes made of gold-and-silver cloth and a horse to ride on up to the king's house, for I am going to marry the princess."

Very well. There was what he wanted in back of the tree yonder; and it was a suit of clothes fit for a great king to wear and a splendid dapple gray horse with a golden saddle and bridle studded all over with precious stones. So Bearskin put on the clothes and rode away, and a fine sight he was to see, I can tell you.

And how the folks stared when he rode up to the king's castle. Out came the king along with the rest, for he thought that Bearskin was some great lord. But the princess knew him the moment she set eyes upon him, for she was not likely to forget him so soon as all that.

The king brought Bearskin into where they were feasting and had a place set for him alongside of himself.

The steward was there along with the rest. "See," said Bearskin to him, "I have a question to put. One killed a dragon and saved a princess, but another came and swore falsely that he did it. Now, what should be done to such a one?"

"Why this," said the steward, speaking up as bold as brass, for he thought he would face the matter down. "He should be put in a cask stuck all round with nails and dragged behind three wild horses."

"Very well," said Bearskin, "you have spoken for yourself. For I killed the dragon up on the hill behind the town, and you stole the glory of the doing."

"That is not so," said the steward, "for it was I who brought home the three heads of the dragon in my own hand. And how can that be with the rest?"

Then Bearskin stepped to the wall, where hung the three heads of the dragon. He opened the mouth of each. "And where are the tongues?" said he.

At this the steward grew as pale as death. Nevertheless he still spoke up as boldly as ever. "Dragons have no tongues," said he. But Bearskin only laughed; he untied his handkerchief before them all, and there were the three tongues. He put one in each mouth, and they fitted exactly, and after that no one could doubt that he was the hero who had really killed the dragon. So when the wedding came, it was Bearskin, and not the steward, who married the princess; what was done to the steward you may guess for yourselves.

And so they had a grand wedding, but in the very midst of the feast one came running in and said there was a great brown bear outside who would come in, willy-nilly. Yes, and you have guessed it right, it *was* the great she-bear, and if nobody else was made much of at that wedding you can depend upon it that she was.

As for the king, he was satisfied that the princess had married a great hero. So she had, only he was the miller's son after all, though the king knew no more of that than my grandfather's little dog, and no more did anybody but the wise man for that matter, and he said nothing of it, for wise folk don't tell all they know.

AFTERWORD

HOWARD PYLE was born in 1853 in Wilmington, Delaware, into a devout Quaker family. He was raised on the Bible, fairy tales and folk stories, and the ballads of Robin Hood, so it is little wonder that when he grew up to be both an author and an illustrator, his three most beloved and successful books were *The Merry Adventures of Robin Hood* (1883), *Pepper & Salt, or Seasoning for Young Folk* (1886), and *The Wonder Clock, or Four and Twenty Marvelous Tales* (1887). These last two were collections of original fairy tales and folk stories created from the author's ever-inventive imagination.

"Bearskin" is the first of the twenty-four stories found in *The Wonder Clock*. Filled with magic, heroic action, and selfless bravery, it is Pyle at his storytelling best. Pyle's childhood exposure to classic tales and the Bible can easily be seen in the first few pages of this story. The huntsman sent off to kill the young babe and bring back its heart as proof of the deed is reminiscent of "Snow White," while putting the infant in a basket made of reeds and setting it adrift on the river echoes the tale of the baby Moses' trip down the Nile. And the great she-bear's adoption of the infant is certainly in the tradition of Romulus and Remus, who were raised by wolves.

But Pyle's genius is that although he starts out with some familiar elements, he soon takes us into a totally new and exciting adventure in which young Bearskin's quick wits and heroic bravery bring him the rewards and happiness he seeks.

In creating new art for this century-old tale, Trina Schart Hyman, like Pyle before her, has taken the story to another level. In her illustrations, we are introduced to a fairy-tale kingdom in which people of different races live, love, work, and play together. Her striking line, bold colors, and joyous good humor leap off the page, inspiring all who visit this fairy-tale realm to strive to make our own everyday world more like it. —*Peter Glassman*